The Secret House

The Secret House

by Carol Beach York

illustrated by Irene Trivas

SCHOLASTIC INC.

New York Toronto London Auckland Sydney

No part of this publication may be reproduced in whole
or in part, or stored in a retrieval system,
or transmitted in any form, or by any means, electronic,
mechanical, photocopying, recording, or otherwise,
without written permission of the publisher.
For information regarding permission, write to
Scholastic Inc., 730 Broadway, New York, NY 10003.

ISBN 0-590-45051-4

Copyright © 1992 by Carol Beach York.
Illustrations copyright © 1992 by Scholastic Inc.
All rights reserved. Published by Scholastic Inc.
APPLE PAPERBACKS is a registered trademark of Scholastic Inc.

12 11 10 9 8 7 6 5 4 3 2 1   2 3 4 5 6 7/9

Printed in the U.S.A.   28

First Scholastic printing, March 1992

For Candy Huckleberry
and her girls,
Terah and Darcy

CONTENTS

The Secret House

On a Dark and Stormy Night

It was a blustery night with no moon or stars to be seen in the sky. Butterfield Square was all gloom and wind and rain. Rain pattered at the windowpanes of the brick houses, on black iron fence railings and brass doorknobs and peaked roofs.

At Number 18, The Good Day Orphanage for Girls, lights glowed at the parlor windows, and everything inside was as bright and cozy as the outside was bleak and cold.

A fire burned in the fireplace, so the parlor was snug and warm on this rainy March night. Winter snows were gone, but it was too soon for spring violets and too soon for buds on trees. It was the changing time — and oh, how the winds did blow!

Around the parlor fire sat the twenty-eight girls who lived at The Good Day.

Little Ann was five, and Elsie May, tall and bossy, was twelve. Everybody else was in between.

Miss Lavender and Miss Plum, the ladies who took care of the girls, loved them all.

Miss Lavender was small and plump, with a pile of white curls on her head. Miss Plum was thin and straight, with kind gray eyes and a bun of hair fastened tight with pins.

Tonight, by the fireside, Miss Plum had agreed to tell a story.

"Make it scary," Phoebe said, as the rain poured at the windows and black night settled down over everything.

"I don't think Miss Plum knows any scary stories," Miss Lavender said, smiling at the thought. Miss Plum would probably tell a nice story about children who were always good, or perhaps about elves and fairies.

"We want a scary story," the other girls began to say.

"Tell a scary story, Miss Plum!"

"A really, really, *really* scary story!"

"All right," Miss Plum said. (Miss Lavender was still sure it would not be very scary. But she was wrong.)

"Once upon a time, on a dark and stormy night," Miss Plum began in a low, mysterious voice.

"A *very* dark and stormy night?" Phoebe asked. She was just-turned-nine and liked everything to be as exciting as possible.

"Yes," said Miss Plum, "a *very* dark and stormy night. In a house — "

"In a house near here?" Elsie May asked. She liked to get everything in order. Was the house near here, or far away in China or Spain?

Miss Plum thought for a moment. Firelight flickered on the faces of all the girls sitting around, waiting for the story: Tatty — not always tidy, though she tried. Kate — the tomboy. Mary and Nonnie. And all the other girls.

4

"Is the house near here?" Elsie May asked again.

At last, slowly and carefully, Miss Plum said, "Yes, in a house near here."

All right, then, thought Elsie May, now they knew where they were.

The other girls just wanted to get on with the story. They sat on the floor around the fire, cross-legged or with their knees drawn up to their chins, waiting to hear what would come next. Little Ann lay on her stomach, close by the fire, warm and happy — and a little scared.

"Well, then," Miss Plum said, beginning again, "on a very dark and stormy night, in a house near here, on a dark and lonely street, a wicked wizard sat in a room deep down below the cellar."

"Below the cellar?" It was Miss Lavender who interrupted now. She had always thought the cellar was as "deep down" as you could go in a house.

"Yes." Miss Plum nodded. "Below the

cellar. He was deep down in the Dark Below."

This made Tatty uneasy, and she moved over closer to the next girl. That was Mary, a girl with red hair who wrote poems; she was thinking of one now, just to herself of course.

O scary night
O scary night
Wizard and cellar
What a fright

"Now in this deep dark room," Miss Plum went on, "a room unknown to anyone else in all the world, the wizard had discovered an old, dusty book. The pages were yellow with age and almost crumbled to dust. However, the wizard could still read some of the words."

"Written in blood?" Phoebe asked.

Miss Plum was startled. Then she said gently, "No, Phoebe, I think written in plain ink."

Not half so exciting, thought Phoebe.

Little Ann watched Miss Plum's face without blinking an eye.

The fire leapt in the fireplace, and the wind rushed about outside, flying through the tree branches, rattling the windows of the houses of Butterfield Square.

"In this ancient book," Miss Plum continued, "were all kinds of magical spells and charms and curses and enchantments. It was called *The Book of Spells*. The wicked wizard wanted to learn all of it, everything in the book. 'I must start from the beginning with something simple,' he said to himself, 'and then something harder and harder, until I've learned it all.'

"He peeked ahead to the last page of the book to see what was the hardest magic of all.

" 'Ah-ha!' he cried when he read that last page, 'when I can do *that*, I shall be the greatest of all the magicians and wizards anywhere!' "

"What was it?"

"What was it?"

"What was it?"

All the girls had the same question.

Miss Plum wouldn't tell. The girls would have to wait until she got to that part of the story.

The Secret House

The Good Day parlor was a lovely, safe, warm place to be hearing a scary story on a dark and stormy night. The clock on the mantel ticked along, and the fire burned brightly in the fireplace, and Miss Plum went on with her story in the bright firelight.

"The wicked wizard, deep down in the Dark Below, thumbed through the withered pages of *The Book of Spells* and tried first one thing and then another. He changed a tiny cellar mouse into a beetle, and it crawled under a bit of earth on the floor and disappeared. The wizard couldn't find any magic to get the mouse back, and that made him rather angry. He turned to another page of the book, found the magic words for making lightning and said them."

"Making lightning?" Miss Lavender mused. "I would have thought that came further along in the book, where the harder things are."

"In this book, there were much harder things," Miss Plum said.

"Now way down in the Dark Below the wizard couldn't hear much. There were no windows, so he couldn't see the sky. So the wizard changed himself into a cat, for speed, and ran up to the cellar, the regular cellar, and then on up into his house. He ran out on his front porch to see if his magic had worked.

"Just as the wizard sprang upon his porch rail, a great crack of lightning came flying out of the sky. It struck the bottom porch step and gouged a great hole and rocked the whole house, and the wicked wizard lifted up his cat-head and howled with delight."

After that, although none of the girls were ready for her to stop, Miss Plum said it was bedtime.

"I'll continue the story tomorrow," she promised.

The twenty-eight girls went upstairs. Several thought they saw a real flash of lightning at the upstairs windows.

When they looked out, they could see only rain pouring down into the darkness of the night.

The next day, walking home from school, Tatty saw a black cat sitting on a porch railing. It was so black, she was sure no one could see it at night, only its two glowing eyes. The cat sat very still with its tail swishing slowly in a rather scary way.

Tatty was walking by herself, a little behind the other Good Day girls. She stopped by the fence and stood looking across the front yard of the house where the cat sat on the porch. The rain of the night before had ended that morning, and the busy March wind had blown things dry. It was a cold day, however, and there was no sunshine. Tatty shivered and held her schoolbooks

closer. She was glad when suddenly Phoebe came along. Tatty thought all the other girls had gone on ahead of her.

"A black cat!" Phoebe noticed at once. She came to a stop by the fence beside Tatty and made another exciting discovery. "Look, Tatty, the bottom porch step has a big hole, just like in Miss Plum's story."

Tatty looked at the porch steps. Yes, there was a splintery, jagged hole right in the middle of the last step.

On the porch rail the black-as-night cat moved its tail with a slow, ominous motion and then rose up silently. As Tatty and Phoebe watched, it sprang down from the porch rail into the yard. It paused for a moment, staring straight at Tatty and Phoebe, and then it began to come toward them, slowly, steadily.

Tatty and Phoebe backed away from the fence cautiously.

"It's the wicked wizard!" Phoebe cried suddenly. "He'll change us into cats, too! Run! *Run!*"

They turned and ran.

Nothing could stop them!

No cat could catch them!

At the corner they slowed down at last, gasping for breath.

"That was the wizard's house," Phoebe declared. "And that was the wizard, changed into a cat. Miss Plum said it was a house near here, remember?"

Phoebe felt thrilled.

They looked back over their shoulders, but bushes growing in front yards along the street cut off their view of the yard where the cat was.

After they walked on a ways, Tatty saw another cat, sitting in a window watching the world go by. It was a calico cat, fluffy and friendly-looking, not at all scary like the black cat. But it was a cat.

"Maybe that wasn't really the wizard's house," Tatty said wisely. "Lots of houses have cats."

Phoebe knew that was true.

She also knew a hole in a porch step

could be made in lots of ways besides a bolt of lightning.

But she didn't want to give up the wicked wizard so quickly.

"We can *pretend* it's his house," she told Tatty. She caught hold of Tatty's arm and made her listen. "Every time we go by, we'll have to be careful he doesn't catch us. We'll have to run by fast every time."

Then they began to run again, pretending the wicked wizard was chasing them.

At The Good Day all the other girls were already in the kitchen having a snack of cocoa and marshmallows from Cook.

Cook was loved by the girls for her snacks — but the snacks were a great source of distress to Mr. Not So Much. Mr. Not So Much was on the Board of Directors of The Good Day, and he came once every month to see that things were going well, although he did not often think they were. He thought he saw too much of everything: food; little blue dresses and little

15

black shoes; flaming fires in winter; ice-cream cones in summer. He wanted to teach Miss Lavender and Miss Plum *economy,* but he had no luck.

Cook liked to make things with raisins *and* nuts *and* brown sugar *and* cherries *and* frosting. This is all very expensive. She kept The Good Day cookie jar full and always gave seconds at dinner. Mr. Not So Much could hardly bear to think of it.

Today, with the cocoa and marshmallows, Cook was also serving fresh bread she had just baked. The whole house was filled with the wonderful smell of just-baked bread.

Miss Plum and Miss Lavender were in the parlor, eating some of this good bread. With the bread they were drinking tea, which they liked better than cocoa — although the girls couldn't understand how this could be. Tea was so *plain.*

Elsie May had not yet rushed starving into the kitchen. She was hanging up her coat in the closet, and the kitchen was her next stop. She was still there in the front hallway when Tatty and Phoebe came in.

Nothing escaped Elsie May. She minded everybody's business and stuck her nose in everywhere.

"What's wrong with you two?" she wanted to know right away. "You're up to something."

Phoebe and Tatty were flushed with the excitement of their escape from the wicked wizard.

"Nothing is wrong," Phoebe answered. She gave Tatty a poke in the back that meant *"Don't tell!"*

Tatty had no intention of telling. She did not tell things to Elsie May.

But Elsie May was staring at her. She wouldn't stop.

Tatty stood somewhat breathlessly, her stockings drooping as usual, and the ribbon gone from her hair. Her coat was buttoned wrong, and arithmetic papers straggled from the edges of her arithmetic book where she had tucked them. She hoped

Miss Lavender and Miss Plum would not ask to see. She had not done very well in class today. The tables of seven did not stay in her mind.

"Stop staring at us," Phoebe told Elsie May in a loud voice.

Elsie May could see she wasn't going to get any information from Phoebe or Tatty, so she said, "Who cares anyway," and went off to the kitchen for her cocoa and bread.

"Never, never tell her," Phoebe warned Tatty in a low voice. "She'll just make fun. We won't tell *anybody*. It will be our secret house," she whispered.

"Can't we just tell Mary?" Tatty asked.

Tatty had been planning to find Mary right away and tell her about the black cat and the hole in the porch step and how they would have to run by fast every day so the wicked wizard wouldn't get them. It was a new game to play, and Tatty thought Mary would want to play, too.

"No!" Phoebe insisted. "If you start telling everybody, it's not a secret anymore."

Time Stops

Just as she promised, Miss Plum continued her story that night.

She began by saying that the wicked wizard didn't think it was very exciting after all to be a cat, not nearly as exciting as he had thought it would be.

"There wasn't much to do, you see," Miss Plum explained. "There wasn't even a mouse to catch. He had changed the cellar mouse into a beetle, and lost it.

" 'I must get back to the book,' the wizard said to himself. He hurried to the deep down Dark Below and changed himself back into a wizard. Then he began looking through *The Book of Spells* again to see what he could do next, and it was really a dreadful thing he found to do."

"*What?*" all the girls asked at once.

"It was a magic powder," Miss Plum said, "and wherever it was sprinkled, time stopped. And that should never be done."

The girls were silent, thinking about what would happen if time stopped.

"Trees and flowers couldn't grow and blossom," Miss Plum said. "Babies would be babies forever. Whomever the powder was sprinkled on would 'stop' and never move again."

"We wouldn't have to go to school," Kate said. That didn't seem so bad.

"You couldn't do *anything*," Miss Plum said.

"You might not miss going to school," Miss Lavender said to Kate, "but you would miss jumping rope and doing cartwheels and having roller-skate races in the park."

"And climbing trees and sliding down banisters and walking on the fence," Elsie May said. These were things Kate was not supposed to do, but sometimes she did.

Elsie May thought Kate should be more la-
dylike.

"Well, wicked though it was," Miss Plum
continued, "the wizard began to mix up
this magic powder. He spent all night mixing it, deep down in the Dark Below."

"How could he see what he was doing?"
Elsie May asked suspiciously.

"He had a candle," Miss Plum said. "The
magic powder was made of secret things
that no one knows, not even me. It had a
very bad smell, and it was a sickly green
color — at least while he was mixing it all
up. When it was mixed, the bad smell faded
some, and the powder lost its green color
and became invisible. That made it all the
more dangerous because no one could see
it.

"It was just getting light outside by the
time the wizard finished mixing all the in-
gredients into the Stop-Time powder.
However, he didn't know that until he
went upstairs into his house. In the Dark

Below it was always nighttime.

"He went into the parlor and pulled up a window shade to let in the light. Then he stood rubbing his bony fingers together, thinking where he would start."

"Did he look like Mr. Not So Much?" Little Ann asked suddenly. Mr. Not So Much was a tall, stern, bony man whose favorite color was black. Bony fingers made her think of Mr. Not So Much.

Miss Plum considered this, and then she said, "He looked a little like Mr. Not So Much, only not quite so tall."

Miss Plum continued. "Of course, the clock was the perfect place to start stopping time. So the wizard sprinkled some powder on the big grandfather clock in the corner of the parlor. He said the magic words that went with the powder . . . something like *abra-ca-dabing, abra-ca-ding* — but not exactly.

"The pendulum of the clock began to swing more and more slowly, and then stopped swinging altogether. The hands of the clock stood still, and not another tick-tock was heard. Then the wizard had an even more wicked idea. His housekeeper was to arrive any minute for her day's work. He decided to sprinkle some Stop-Time powder on her to see if it would work on live things.

"While he waited for his housekeeper, he lifted the cover of the birdcage where the housekeeper kept a pretty yellow canary. It sang to her while she did her housekeeping. But now the canary was sound asleep on one foot with its head under its wing.

"The wizard sprinkled the canary with his powder and put the cover back on the cage. At last he heard the housekeeper coming in the kitchen door.

" 'I'm going to fix your breakfast,' the housekeeper said. That was always the first thing she did every morning."

"What did the wizard eat?" Mary asked. She raised her hand to ask, like she did at school. She forgot where she was.

"The wizard ate raw eggs that were no

longer fresh, and curdled milk, and nothing you would like," Miss Plum said. "His housekeeper had to fix the breakfast with a clothespin on her nose. Old eggs and sour milk do not smell pleasant.

"By and by the housekeeper came into the parlor with his breakfast tray.

"In a sweet voice, he said, 'Do sit down a minute, my dear.' He had never before called her 'my dear.'

"The poor lady's feet hurt, and she was glad to sit down whenever she could.

"She had hardly sat down in a parlor chair when the wizard said his magic words and threw a sprinkle of Stop-Time powder on her head. Some got up her nose, but before she could even sneeze she was 'stopped.' She sat in her chair, still as the clock.

"The wizard was delighted. He ate his breakfast and rushed back downstairs into the cellar room to see what he could try next from the ancient, evil book . . .

". . . and I will tell you more tomorrow."

"Oh, please, more, more," begged Elsie Mae.

Phoebe and Tatty joined the other girls in asking, "More, please, more."

"That's enough for tonight," said Miss Plum with a nod of her head.

Clock, Bird, and Head

The next morning on the way to school there was no chance for Tatty and Phoebe to lag behind the other girls, or linger at the secret house.

"Don't dawdle," Miss Plum always said when the girls left for school.

Tatty and Phoebe hurried along with the other girls, just giving the old house a passing glance as though it didn't mean anything special to them.

After school, feeling important and mysterious, Tatty and Phoebe stayed behind in the school yard. They played on the teeter-totter until everybody else was gone. They planned to walk home past their secret house and see what they could see, and then run away as fast as they could run.

The front porch of the house was empty, and there was a dismal, lonely look all about. Because the cat had scared them away so fast the day before, they hadn't noticed how old and shabby the house was. Weedy winter grass was a dingy yellow-brown in the yard, and nobody had fixed the hole in the porch step.

The girls forgot they were going to run away fast.

"There's no cat," Tatty whispered.

She didn't know right away if this was good or bad.

Phoebe knew. She knew right away and without any doubt that now this really might be the wizard's house. "There's no cat because the wizard changed himself back, remember?"

Tatty stood staring at the silent, shabby house where there was no sign of anything or anybody, not even the cat. "That's only pretend," she reminded Phoebe. "Maybe the cat is inside the house today."

Even so, Tatty began to have a funny feeling about the house. What if they really had found the wizard's house, and inside was a bony man — not quite as tall as Mr. Not So Much — eating raw old eggs and curdled milk . . . while in the parlor . . . well, Tatty didn't like to think about that part.

"Let's just sneak up a minute and peek in," Phoebe said. She glanced around to see if anybody was watching. A few cars were driving by, and across the street a woman was bringing home groceries in a brown paper bag. Nobody was watching Phoebe and Tatty.

"Come on," Phoebe urged. "Let's peek in."

Tatty thought that was an awful idea.

"Oh, Phoebe," she said, with a gasp of surprise. "We can't peek in somebody's house."

"This isn't just *somebody's* house," Phoebe said. "This is the wicked wizard's house."

"Maybe not," Tatty said faintly.

"Well, *I'm* going to look in," said Phoebe.

She felt very brave and daring. Let Tatty run home if she wanted to; *she* was going to have a look! She opened the front gate, which creaked just the way a gate to a wicked wizard's house should creak. Perfect, thought Phoebe. And as though she lived there, up the walk she went. Tatty felt odd standing alone on the sidewalk, so she crept after Phoebe, clutching her schoolbooks and chewing her lip.

The porch stairs creaked. All the more perfect, thought Phoebe. They both stepped carefully to avoid the lightning hole and saw one window with a raised shade. Phoebe leaned close and peered inside. Tatty stood at the top of the porch steps and would not go any closer just then.

The window was not very clean, but Phoebe could see into the room by pressing her nose against the glass and squinting.

The room was a small parlor, quiet and deserted. Phoebe looked all around, and then — she caught her breath! There in a corner was a stopped clock. She could see the pendulum hanging straight down and still. The hands pointed to ten minutes past seven, which was surely not the time now. School let out at three o'clock, and they had only played on the teeter-totter for a few minutes. And then! Phoebe saw a birdcage, covered with a piece of green checkered cloth. Oh, how she wished she could see if under the cover was a yellow bird on one foot with its head under its wing, stopped in time.

"Tatty — Tatty — come here!" Phoebe called from the window. "Come and see what's in here. Come and see, come and see!"

Tatty crept forward a step or two.

Phoebe pushed Tatty's face close to the window, and Tatty saw for herself the stopped clock and the silent, covered, mysterious birdcage.

She also saw a head. It was sticking up over the back of a chair. She could see just a round top with gray hair. The head did not move.

"The lady's there — the housekeeper," Tatty said, her voice hushed with awe. She edged away from the window fearfully, and Phoebe pressed her nose again to look.

Yes, Tatty was right. Phoebe, too, could see the top of the housekeeper's head at the back of a chair, where she sat stopped forever in time.

They ran back down the porch steps, and ran all the way to the corner before they stopped.

"Maybe it's just someone fallen asleep." Tatty was panting as she tried to talk.

Phoebe didn't want to hear this. Their secret house *was* the wicked wizard's house, Phoebe was sure.

"Now, remember, it's our secret," Phoebe reminded Tatty as they walked on toward The Good Day.

It was a harder secret to keep now, Tatty

thought. The secret house seemed real, like the real wizard's house, and not pretend anymore. It was too much of a secret for Tatty to hold. She wished she could tell someone.

Phoebe was delighted with the secret. Wild horses couldn't drag it out of her!

The Stone Boy

Miss Plum had promised to go on with the story of the wizard, and just before bedtime all the girls gathered in the parlor again to hear what the wicked wizard would try next from *The Book of Spells*.

"I feel like Sheherazade," Miss Plum said. She took her seat in a chair by the fireplace and crossed her ankles.

"Who was Sheher—Sheher—who was *that?*" Kate gave up trying to say the name right. It was certainly nobody *she* knew.

"Sheherazade was the wife of the King of Samarkand, and she told him a story every night for a thousand and one nights, to save her life. As long as she had another story to tell, the King let her live."

The girls all thought the King of Samarkand did not sound very nice.

"Wasn't it hard for her to make up so many stories?" Tatty asked. Sometimes at school Teacher would ask the class to write a story, and Tatty never knew what to write.

"I think if your life were at stake, you would make up stories rather quickly," Miss Plum said, and Miss Lavender agreed. She nodded her head and bounced her curls. "Yes, indeed," she said.

Again there was a flickering fire, and the night outside was very dark; there was no moon in the sky over Butterfield Square. While the girls sat in their cozy parlor, the wizard was once more in his deep dark cellar, turning the pages of his book.

"Stopping time no longer interested the wizard," Miss Plum said. "He found it rather boring; nothing happened, and he had to fix his own meals because the housekeeper was stopped in her chair.

"So he undid the Stop-Time magic and

went back to his book. He wanted to skip right to the last page then and there, but in his wicked heart he knew he wasn't ready yet. He contented himself with earlier pages. This time he came upon a page that told about using plants from the forest to make potions that would cause enchantments and spells and terrible curses to befall people."

Little Ann was not sure what all that meant.

"What kind of spells and enchantments and curses?" Elsie May asked.

"Potions to make beautiful women into horrible hags," Miss Plum explained. "To turn people into statues, or into owls and spiders and snakes."

"Oh, yuk!" Elsie May said, twisting a long yellow braid and wrinkling her nose.

"Or elephants?" asked Little Ann.

"Into anything he wanted, I expect," Miss Plum said. "Or put them to sleep for a thousand years, or make their ears grow big and all their teeth fall out."

At the sound of these horrible fates, the girls grew very silent.

"So the wizard went off in the dead of night to the farthest-most hidden part of the forest, where the poison plants grew — the nightshade and henbane and foxglove and laurel and laburnum and yew. Forest animals watched him, their eyes shining in the darkness. The wizard could hear them skittering around, sneaking behind him, rustling in the leaves. It was a dark and spooky old place, indeed, where the poison plants grew. No one had ever been in that hidden part of the forest before. The wizard was the first one.

"He gathered a basketful of plants and went back to his house. While it was still dark, hurrying to be finished before the first rays of morning light came, the wizard planted the plants in his own backyard. Now he would have his own garden of plants for making the magic potions.

"He took a few plants into his deep down Dark Below and began mixing up a few potions right away. He couldn't see it, of course, but outside the sky was beginning to get a tinge of pink where the sun was coming up.

"When he went upstairs at last, he looked out of the kitchen window and saw a boy in the middle of his new garden.

" 'What are you doing in my garden!' the wizard called out. He went into the garden angrily, shaking his fist at the poor boy.

" 'My ball bounced into your yard,' the boy explained. 'I'm looking for it.'

" 'You're lying!' the wizard accused. But the boy was really telling the truth.

"Then suddenly the wizard changed his manner. 'Let me help you look for your ball,' he said kindly. He pretended to look all around, under the bushes, behind the trees, along the straggly, ugly rows of poison plants he had brought from the forest.

"When the wizard found the ball behind

a bush, he hid it in his own pocket. He pretended to go on looking, as he said, 'Where can that ball be?'

"The boy looked, too; but finally they had to give up.

" 'Let me get you something refreshing to drink,' the wizard said. Then he brought out a glass filled with one of the potions he had prepared, and he gave it to the boy to drink.

"Oh, it tasted delicious, and the boy drank it down in one long gulp and handed back the glass. He wanted to ask for more, but he couldn't speak. He had turned to stone, right where he stood."

Little Ann put her head on her arm and gazed at Miss Plum sadly.

None of the girls said anything for a few moments.

"Real stone?" Phoebe asked finally.

"I'm afraid so," Miss Plum said. "He was a very wicked wizard."

"I hope he'll come to a bad end," Miss Lavender muttered to herself.

Miss Plum heard, and smiled a wise smile. "We shall see," she said.

Nobody could get her to say another word about the story that night.

Phoebe and Tatty shared a bedroom with Mary. As they got ready for bed that night, Phoebe whispered to Tatty about the secret house. She didn't want Mary to hear.

"What if we find poison plants and a boy changed to a statue?"

Phoebe was thrilled, but a little anxious.

Tatty was *very* anxious. She was beginning not to like the secret house very much. It was a mysterious, gloomy old house and she was glad she didn't have to live there. As for finding poison plants and a boy changed to stone . . . Tatty got into her bed and thought about that and felt more and more anxious.

Phoebe, too, thought about the wizard and the secret house before she fell asleep. Now the house was less and less pretend. It was almost truly the wizard's, and she wondered if she would find a garden of strange forest plants and a boy turned to stone in the backyard. She would have to be brave enough to go into the backyard to look.

Mary slept peacefully because nobody had told her the secret, and she had nothing to worry about.

The next afternoon Tatty and Phoebe stood again by the gate of the secret house.

They wondered whether they dared to sneak around and take a look at the backyard. Tatty was sure Miss Plum and Miss Lavender would not approve of going into strange yards — even if they were brave enough.

It was still very much March. Gusty winds scurried around everywhere, disturbing people's hats and tossing scraps of paper along the curbs. Wind lifted Tatty's hair and blew it across her face. Wind flapped at Phoebe's blue Good Day skirt and made her legs shivery with cold.

At last they went cautiously up the stone path toward the house, and followed the path around the house to the backyard. There were some straggly plants by the back steps, although Tatty and Phoebe didn't know if they were nightshade and henbane and all the other names Miss Plum had said.

But they certainly knew a statue when they saw one, and there in the very middle of the garden was a stone boy — standing very straight and holding out his hand.

Phoebe and Tatty huddled together at the corner of the house and stared at the stone boy.

Mrs. Bennett, who lived next door to The Good Day, had two flamingos made of pink plastic in her flower garden. At a house across the street from The Good Day was a birdbath with a stone bird perched on the rim. Another house Tatty and Phoebe knew about had a stone swan sitting by the flowerpots at the door.

These were garden decorations. And now here was another.

"What if it's a real boy?" Tatty whispered — and then they turned and ran back around the house, and were almost to the safety of the street when Phoebe stopped, took a deep breath to get courage, and ran back to the house and up the front porch steps.

After a quick look into the parlor windows, she came flying through the yard.

Tatty was already on the sidewalk waiting, breathless and panting.

"The clock's going!" Phoebe reported all-in-a-rush as she joined Tatty. "The spell of stopping time is broken — and the lady and the bird are gone, I don't know where, and the clock is swinging."

She had seen the glint of the pendulum behind the glass and seen the steady, rhythmic move from side to side as it swung.

Phoebe was sure now beyond any doubt

that their secret house was the wicked wizard's house, and she was sorry she didn't have a magic potion that would bring the stone boy back to life. It would have been a good deed to do.

To Tell or Not to Tell

When Tatty and Phoebe got back to The Good Day, Miss Lavender was just waking from a nap.

"My goodness, I've overslept," she said to herself, yawning and blinking as she sat up. She had pulled her window shades partly down, and the room was dim and sleepy and had soft shadows in the corners. She felt greatly refreshed from her nap.

Outside, the March afternoon was drawing to an end. It was cold, and the wind was rising; night was near.

When Miss Lavender came downstairs, she found Tatty and Phoebe sitting on the bottom step in the front hall. They still had on their coats and still held their schoolbooks in their arms. They still felt shaky after seeing the stone boy.

"Is everything all right?" Miss Lavender peered at their serious faces.

Phoebe nodded brightly and managed a smile. Tatty longed to tell Miss Lavender about the secret house. She didn't want to have a secret any longer. But she felt Phoebe's elbow pressing against her, so she kept silent.

Miss Lavender went down the hall into the parlor. It was empty. Miss Plum had returned from shopping and was sorting out the parcels she had bought: new stockings for the girls, sewing thread for Miss Lavender, a packet of "Plant Green" for the fern in the hall, and some writing paper in a shiny blue box. These interesting things soon took Miss Lavender's mind from everything else.

Back on the hall stairs, Tatty and Phoebe still had their problem.

"I want to tell Mary," Tatty begged. "I want to tell *somebody*."

"Well, all right," Phoebe agreed at last.

She knew Mary could keep a secret. "But only Mary."

They went to find her.

Mary was upstairs in her room, which was also Tatty's and Phoebe's room, learning her spelling words. She sat at the table by the window, in a wooden chair painted blue. There were two other chairs at the table, one was Tatty's and one was Phoebe's. Tatty's chair was blue like Mary's chair, and Phoebe's was red and had a cushion she had made herself, with hardly any lumps in the stuffing.

There were three beds in the room, each in a corner, and a cupboard to keep toys and books. In the closet was a paper wreath the girls had made to hang in their window every Christmas — if it lasted, being only paper.

Mary was wide-eyed with surprise to hear about the secret house.

A black cat and a hole in the step made by lightning?

A room where time had stopped?

A garden of evil plants and a boy turned to stone?

It was hard to believe!

"Tomorrow you can come with us after school," Tatty said. "We'll show you."

Poor Mary, how would she get to sleep tonight after hearing all this? Spelling words left her mind — perhaps forever.

All Into Gold

The twenty-eight girls and Miss Plum and Miss Lavender were once again gathered around the warm fire in the parlor. It was too bad Mr. Not So Much was not at The Good Day that evening when Miss Plum resumed her story. He would have liked what happened next. The wizard discovered a formula for turning everything into gold.

"It didn't matter what it was," Miss Plum said. "Wood, brick, glass, tin, feather, fur, or flesh; he could turn everything into gold."

Mr. Not So Much would have slapped the wizard on the back and become his friend at once.

"The wizard had a Midas touch, so to speak — " Right there Miss Plum stopped for a minute to say that Midas was a king who could turn things into gold just by touching them.

"The wizard had to say magic words," Miss Plum explained, "and tap three times with his magic wand, but things changed to gold so it amounted to the same thing in the end."

"When the wizard found out he could do that, he thought it must surely be the most important thing in *The Book of Spells* — except the last page, of course. He cared no more for magic plants and he wanted to turn the stone boy in his garden into a gold boy, which was much more valuable. So he hurried up from his deep cellar room."

Tatty and Phoebe looked at each other uneasily. They began to have very funny feelings about not telling. They should have told someone about the boy in the garden.

Miss Plum was going on with the story.

"First the wizard changed the boy back to a real boy. He decided he would make the boy work awhile first, and then he would change him into gold.

"He told the boy to go into the kitchen and fix the eggs and curdled milk for breakfast. You see, the housekeeper had taken her canary and gone away and never come back after the wizard made the Stop-Time powder. She didn't want to work for anyone who played tricks like that.

"Of course the boy didn't want to work for somebody who changed him into stone. When the wizard went back to the cellar to wait for his breakfast, the boy ran right out the back door and was never seen by the wizard again. The boy's mother was very happy when he came home, for she had missed him."

Tatty and Phoebe — and Mary, too — all breathed great sighs of relief to hear that the stone boy had escaped. He was a real boy again, and was also safe from being turned to gold. Gold is pretty to look at, but it is not as wonderful as a real, live person.

"The wizard was extremely angry when he discovered that the boy was gone. However, there was nothing he could do about it. He went all around his house changing everything into gold, all the chairs and tables and knickknacks — ”

“Did he have knickknacks?” Miss Lavender looked up from her mending. She liked to keep busy while she listened to the story, and mending at The Good Day never ended.

“None you would like,” Miss Plum replied, glancing around at the pretty things in the parlor: the mantel ornaments and the lovely mantel clock, the china lady on the piano, the brass swan on the windowsill, the trinkets on the desk. “The wizard’s knickknacks were bits of bones and a stuffed bat, things like that.”

“I couldn’t live in a house with a stuffed bat,” Miss Lavender said quickly.

“Or a live one,” Miss Plum added. “Even worse.”

“My goodness, yes.” Miss Lavender felt a bit pale to think of a live bat in the house.

“As the wizard was changing everything

in his house to gold, he was hoping some-one would knock at his door so he could try his golden touch on a real person," Miss Plum went on.

"He pulled down all the window shades so that no one could see into his house and try to steal his gold . . . and I will continue the story tomorrow."

"Oh, please tell us more now!" the girls begged.

But Miss Plum only laughed.

"No more tonight," she said. "Tomorrow I will end the story, and you will find out what was on the last page, what was the final thing the wizard tried from *The Book of Spells*."

The Golden Windows

The next afternoon was Mary's first time to go to the secret house with Phoebe and Tatty.

She thought about it all afternoon at school, and once Teacher had to say, "Mary, you are not paying attention." Which was certainly true. Mary's mind was on things other than a geography lesson. Her map of Europe did not turn out right at all — Italy looked like a thin snake dangling down into the Mediterranean.

Spelling did not go well, either.

At last school was over, and Mary lingered with Tatty and Phoebe in the school yard, to let the other girls go on ahead. The school yard seemed strange when everybody had gone. Mary had never been the last to leave.

Finally Phoebe bounced off the teeter-totter and said, "Let's go!"

When they got to the secret house, they stood by the gate and didn't go even one step into the yard.

The shades were drawn down at all the windows, but not far enough to hide what was inside. *All the windows of the house glimmered gold.*

Tatty and Phoebe and Mary stared with awe.

It truly was the wicked wizard's house . . . wasn't it?

"Maybe it's only the sun," Mary whispered at last.

The week had been so cloudy, this was the first time Tatty and Phoebe had seen the secret house on a sunny day. If it was the sun, it didn't seem to be shining on the windows of the other houses in quite the same way.

But some of the houses were shaded by trees, so it was hard to tell.

They wanted to go into the backyard and

see if the stone boy was really gone. But if the wizard was waiting behind his door for a live person to come along, they didn't want to be caught and changed into gold. Not even Phoebe would go up on the porch to peek in a window.

They left at last, running off as hard as they could in case the wizard had seen them and was coming after them.

Tatty looked back once, and the windows were still golden.

The Last Page

That night Miss Plum's story came to an end.

The girls sat on the floor by the fire, hugging their knees, silent as mice. They didn't want to miss a word. Tatty and Phoebe and Mary sat together in a huddle, more concerned than anybody else in the whole room.

Little Ann lay on her stomach. Miss Lavender took up her mending. The fire leapt behind the grate.

Miss Plum began.

" 'I've learned enough,' the wizard decided, deep down in the Dark Below. He flipped straight to the last page of his old, crumbling *Book of Spells*. And what do you think he found there?"

Miss Plum looked around at her audience, and all the girls began to guess.

"A magic thing to make trees talk?"

"A spell to make him grow into a giant?"

"A way to walk through walls, like a ghost?"

"A spell to make himself invisible?"

"A spell to turn people into elephants?" said Little Ann.

Miss Plum shook her head at every guess.

"What the wizard found on the last page of the book was a magic blueprint for a sort of spaceship that would carry him into outer space. He wanted to find the witches and wizards and magicians and sorcerers who lived on faraway stars, and threw down thunderbolts, and pulled dark clouds over the moon, and sent down rain and hail and blew up the winds. Then he would brew great storms and declare himself king of all the wizards.

"First the wizard made everything in his house disappear. He was so selfish, he didn't want people to have all his golden things after he was gone. He tore up all the magic plants in his garden, so no one could have those, either.

"Then he built the spaceship in the dark of night. Part of the ship he built down in his deep down Dark Below, and when it was getting too large for the room, he brought it up to the back porch.

"He worked hard to get the spaceship built before morning.

"It was still dark night when he finished his work and set off at last with a great fiery blast, zooming into the sky."

"Did he find the other witches and wizards?" Kate asked.

"No, he never found anybody," Miss Plum said, smiling. "He had been so busy getting rid of his gold so no one could have it, and tearing up his garden (though not many people would want those awful plants), and so busy rushing to get his spaceship built, that he blasted off without a map of the stars. And so he got lost right away before he was even up very far. He

kept going, hoping he would find someone or something, and he kept getting farther and farther into space and more and more hopelessly lost.

"He will probably be circling up there forever and ever. He can't do anybody any harm that way, which is a good thing."

And that was the end of the story.

Little Ann was sleepy now, her eyelids drooping. The fire felt so warm.

"I like happy endings," Kate said.

Miss Lavender snipped a thread and put her mending away for the night. She liked happy endings, too, although she was still surprised that Miss Plum knew such a scary story.

Phoebe and Tatty and Mary were wondering about the secret house. Was it really empty now? Was the wizard gone? They could hardly wait to see.

After they went to bed that night, all the girls thought about the wicked wizard roaming forever through the universe, not able to do any more wicked things.

It was the best ending ever for a story.

The next morning, Miss Plum stood by the front door to give the girls their last-minute going-to-school inspection.

All looked in good order.

. . . Well, Tatty's hair was in her eyes again, and her stockings were drooping. But that was often the case.

Miss Plum hoped Kate would get to school without finding a tree to climb . . .

. . . and that nobody would chew gum —
— or forget to be polite.

Elsie May walked along with her nose in the air.

Little Ann ran to keep up.

And by and by, they were all out of sight.

Miss Plum went to the parlor, where Miss Lavender was drinking a cup of tea she had brought from the breakfast table. Cook was busy with breakfast dishes in her kitchen, and all was peaceful at The Good Day.

But at school, the girls were not at peace. All day Phoebe fussed in her seat. She thought the school clock had stopped — like the clock in the wizard's house.

Tatty forgot her tables of sevens again, and Mary kept going off into dazes. "You are not concentrating," Teacher said to her.

Finally, *finally,* school was over. Phoebe and Tatty and Mary stayed in the playground until the other girls had gone.

Then they went to the secret house.

Across the drab winter grass of the front yard they saw the house, bleak and desolate and as gray as the cloudy sky above.

The house had a definite look of emptiness, they thought.

For a minute or two, they stood absolutely still at the edge of the yard.

"I'm going to look inside," Phoebe said at last. She had to *know.*

She opened the creaky gate and went into the yard and up the porch steps. Tatty and Mary came cautiously behind, stepping carefully around the lightning hole.

The shades were drawn down at the windows — but one shade had not been drawn all the way. There was an inch or two of bare window at the bottom, and Phoebe squinted her eyes and peered in. She could see the parlor, where the grandfather clock had stood in a corner and there had been a birdcage and the head of somebody sitting in a chair that had its back to the window.

Now Phoebe saw only a bare, deserted room.

There was nothing. No lamp, table, book, chair, cupboard, or carpet.

"Everything's gone," Phoebe reported with awe. "Look."

Tatty and Mary got very brave and peeked into the wizard's parlor.

Just as Phoebe had said, everything was gone.

It was a scary moment. They knew now for sure that they had found the wizard's house.

It was also a happy moment. Miss Plum had said the wizard was gone, gone forever into outer space. There was no danger here now.

Phoebe led the way as they all raced down the porch steps and around the side of the house to the backyard.

The stone boy was gone, safely home again!

The poison plants had been dug up and only bare, gouged dirt lay at the back porch steps.

On the steps were bits of sawdust and a few leftover nails.

Somebody had been building something . . . building a spaceship.

Phoebe and Tatty and Mary looked up into the sky, where the wizard had flown into a dark night and forever lost his way among the stars.

Deep Down in the Dark Below

Every day Tatty and Phoebe and Mary walked by the secret house on their way home from school.

Nothing changed.

The house stood deserted and shabby, with the lightning hole in the front porch step and the torn-up garden in the backyard and the dull March sky overhead.

But spring *was* coming.

A forsythia bush began to bud in the corner of The Good Day yard.

The skies were less gray, and the wind less blustery, although children were still trying to fly kites and grown-ups still carried umbrellas in case of rain.

Crocuses came up in the Butterfield

Square park, and girls ran out to play without caps or mittens.

Roller-skate races began on the sidewalks, and Miss Plum handed out jump ropes and chalk for hopscotch.

And then one day, about two weeks after the wizard had gone off into space, new people moved into the secret house. Tatty and Phoebe and Mary were just coming by on their way home from school, and they saw a large red moving van parked by the curb.

Husky men were moving in furniture, and it was very interesting to watch.

There was a bookcase with glass doors, and a comfortable-looking sofa upholstered in green velvet. So the girls knew the new people liked to read books and to be comfortable.

There were lamps and tables and pictures for the walls.

There was a baby's crib and a rocking horse and a tiny rocking chair.

"They've got a baby," Tatty whispered. She hoped a baby would be safe in a wizard's house.

"He's gone," Phoebe reminded her, and then Tatty felt better.

There were boxes of books for the bookcase.

Boxes of china for the kitchen, where only raw eggs and curdled milk had once been served.

A large box of glass jars for canning jellies and jams.

"Let's ask Miss Plum what happened to the wizard's house in the story," Tatty said.

"This *is* the wizard's house." Phoebe was amazed that Tatty could still doubt.

Tatty tugged up a drooping stocking. "I just thought we could ask. Then we'd be sure."

Phoebe shook her head. "She'd want to know why we were asking. We can't say it's because we saw new people moving into a a house where we peeked through windows."

Mary thought Phoebe was right, they shouldn't ask.

So they didn't.

The new people fixed the porch step and gave the house a coat of fresh white paint. The house began to look tidy and cheerful. Mary said the people would probably plant flowers in the summer; you could tell they wanted to make the house as pretty as possible.

Tatty still wanted to know what happened to the wizard's house in the story, but she didn't ask.

I'll never know, she thought. I'll never know for sure.

Then one morning, between the orange juice and the oatmeal at breakfast, Little Ann tugged at Miss Plum's sleeve. Her chair was next to Miss Plum's chair at the table.

"What happened to the wizard's house after he went away?"

It was like a miracle to Tatty.

"Well, let me think." Miss Plum was thoughtful for a moment.

Phoebe and Mary looked at each other across the table.

They looked at Tatty.

Tatty looked at them.

Everyone was quiet.

"*I* was wondering about that all along," Elsie May said, to show she was really the smartest.

"By and by, a very nice family moved into the house," Miss Plum said. "A mother and father and baby. And they are very happy there."

"Did they ever find the Dark Below?" Kate leaned forward in her chair to look down the table toward Miss Plum.

"Yes, they did, almost right away," Miss Plum nodded.

"I don't suppose they liked it much, way down there." Miss Lavender shivered. "I wouldn't."

"Oh, they cleaned it up and swept it out

until it was a nice tidy snug little room," Miss Plum said. *"The Book of Spells* crumbled to dust when they picked it up — and that was the end of *that*.

"The mother of the family is going to use the room to store the jars of jellies and jams she likes to make.

"And that is the whole story."

About the Author

Carol Beach York began writing poetry and short stories at age seven, and by the time she was ten, wrote her first full-length book. She still keeps the original plain brown composition book in which she wrote her first book, an adventure story.

Since then, Carol has written a variety of best-selling books, including mysteries, fantasies, stories of the supernatural, and romances. She says, "The most pleasurable experiences I have are with the Good Day Orphanage. I am at home with everybody. Writing these stories is like recording what is happening; the characters are acting for me. I love them all, even Mr. Not So Much."

Carol enjoys reading books, especially old books, as well as writing them. She lives in Chicago, Illinois, and has one daughter. Among her best-selling and well-loved stories are *Rabbit Magic*, *Good Charlotte*, *The Christmas Dolls*, and *Kate Be Late*.

LITTLE ● APPLE ®

B A B Y · S I T T E R S
Little Sister ™
by Ann M. Martin, author of *The Baby-sitters Club* ®

❑	MQ44300-3	#1	Karen's Witch	$2.75
❑	MQ44259-7	#2	Karen's Roller Skates	$2.75
❑	MQ44299-6	#3	Karen's Worst Day	$2.75
❑	MQ44264-3	#4	Karen's Kittycat Club	$2.75
❑	MQ44258-9	#5	Karen's School Picture	$2.75
❑	MQ44298-8	#6	Karen's Little Sister	$2.75
❑	MQ44257-0	#7	Karen's Birthday	$2.75
❑	MQ42670-2	#8	Karen's Haircut	$2.75
❑	MQ43652-X	#9	Karen's Sleepover	$2.75
❑	MQ43651-1	#10	Karen's Grandmothers	$2.75
❑	MQ43650-3	#11	Karen's Prize	$2.75
❑	MQ43649-X	#12	Karen's Ghost	$2.75
❑	MQ43648-1	#13	Karen's Surprise	$2.75
❑	MQ43646-5	#14	Karen's New Year	$2.75
❑	MQ43645-7	#15	Karen's in Love	$2.75
❑	MQ43644-9	#16	Karen's Goldfish	$2.75
❑	MQ43643-0	#17	Karen's Brothers	$2.75
❑	MQ43642-2	#18	Karen's Home-Run	$2.75
❑	MQ43641-4	#19	Karen's Good-Bye	$2.75
❑	MQ44823-4	#20	Karen's Carnival	$2.75
❑	MQ44824-2	#21	Karen's New Teacher	$2.75
❑	MQ44833-1	#22	Karen's Little Witch	$2.75
❑	MQ44832-3	#23	Karen's Doll	$2.75
❑	MQ44859-5	#24	Karen's School Trip	$2.75
❑	MQ44831-5	#25	Karen's Pen Pal	$2.75
❑	MQ44830-7	#26	Karen's Ducklings	$2.75
❑	MQ44829-3	#27	Karen's Big Joke	$2.75
❑	MQ44828-5	#28	Karen's Tea Party	$2.75
❑	MQ44825-0	#29	Karen's Cartwheel	$2.75
❑	MQ43647-3		Karen's Wish Super Special #1	$2.95
❑	MQ44834-X		Karen's Plane Trip Super Special #2	$2.95
❑	MQ44827-7		Karen's Mystery Super Special #3	$2.95

Available wherever you buy books, or use this order form.

Scholastic Inc., P.O. Box 7502, 2931 E. McCarty Street, Jefferson City, MO 65102

Please send me the books I have checked above. I am enclosing $_____ (please add $2.00 to cover shipping and handling). Send check or money order - no cash or C.O.Ds please.

Name_____

Address_____

City_____ State/Zip_____

Please allow four to six weeks for delivery. Offer good in U.S.A. only. Sorry, mail orders are not available to residents to Canada. Prices subject to change.

BLS991